TO GILLIAN, SARAH AND BENJAMIN

Text and illustrations copyright © 1999 by Gary Clement
First paperback edition published in Canada and the USA in 2010
by Groundwood Books

Groundwood Books / House of Anansi Press
110 Spadina Avenue, Suite 801, Toronto, Ontario M5V 2K4
or c/o Publishers Group West
1700 Fourth Street, Berkeley, CA 94710

We acknowledge for their financial support of our publishing
program the Canada Council for the Arts, the Government of Canada
through the Canada Book Fund (CBF) and the Ontario Arts Council.

Library and Archives Canada Cataloguing in Publication

Clement, Gary
The Great Poochini / written and illustrated by Gary Clement.
ISBN 978-0-88899-990-0
I. Title.
PS8555.L398G73 2010   jC813'.54   C2009-906510-X

Design by Alysia Shewchuk
Printed and bound in China

The
GREAT
POOCHINI

WRITTEN AND ILLUSTRATED BY

GARY CLEMENT

GROUNDWOOD BOOKS / HOUSE OF ANANSI PRESS
TORONTO BERKELEY

I t is three o'clock in the afternoon, and Signor Poochini is standing on a Persian rug in the center of a softly lit parlor performing some very important vocal exercises.

"La, la, la, la, la, la, la," he sings delicately.

"Mi, mi, mi, mi, mi, mi," he utters sweetly.

"So, so, so, so, so, so," he declares forcefully.

Tonight is the premiere of the opera, Dog Giovanni, by the legendary composer, Wolfhound Amadeus Mozart. It will take place at the famed Muttropolitan Opera House, and Signor Poochini will be singing the title role.

As you can plainly see, Signor Poochini is no ordinary dog. He is handsome, housebroken and hounded by throngs of adoring fans. He is, in fact, the Great Poochini, the most renowned opera-singing dog of his generation and, some say, the finest canine lyric tenor ever to have graced the opera stage.

Signor Poochini lives with a man named Hersh in a big old three-story house with a small yard on a shady street in the heart of a big city.

When Signor Poochini is with Hersh, he does ordinary dog things.

He barks and buries bones.

He chases cars and cats.

He fetches balls and branches.

Together, Signor Poochini and Hersh like to take long walks, eat hearty foods and, yes, listen to the opera.

Hersh calls Signor Poochini Jack.

Of course, Hersh has absolutely no idea that Signor Poochini is a great star of the opera.

How could he?

Signor Poochini only sings late at night, in a secret part of town that only opera-loving dogs know.

Every night, Signor Poochini waits until Hersh is fast asleep. Then he leaps, smoothly and cleanly, through the bedroom window. Hersh always leaves that window open, even in winter.

"The night air cures whatever ails you, Jackie boy," Hersh always says.

It is four o'clock in the afternoon and Signor Poochini has now finished his vocal exercises. His voice needs a rest and so does his body. He will have a short nap and then, if time permits, a light snack at a quiet bistro. Perhaps just a small plate of Fettuccine Arfredo and a glass of Dog Perignon, or maybe just a nice piece of hound cake.

Then, it's off to the theater.

As Signor Poochini pads over to his bed, Hersh enters the room. He scratches Signor Poochini behind the ears and says, "I'm going to my sister's tonight, Jack. There's food and drink on the table and snacks in the pantry. I'll be back bright and early tomorrow morning to fix us a nourishing breakfast."

Signor Poochini softly barks goodbye to Hersh as the door shuts. Then he settles down for his nap.

When Signor Poochini awakens, it is already dark. He glances at the clock and sees that tonight's performance begins in less than an hour.

Signor Poochini decides to skip the bistro and instead rush directly to the theater.

"No time to lose," he thinks as he scrambles into Hersh's bedroom. Signor Poochini looks up as he approaches the window and finds it . . . closed, shut tight, completely sealed.

"Horrors," gasps Signor Poochini. "The window is locked and Hersh won't be back until the morning."

Signor Poochini paces and thinks, thinks and paces.

"Miss the premiere," he grumbles. "Why, it's preposterous. It's . . . it's unthinkable. It's . . . it's . . . it's impossible!"

And yet, there seems to be no way out for Signor Poochini.

As the clock ticks away, the cream of dog society begins to assemble in the theater lobby. Everywhere you look — furs and finery, bow wows and bow ties, top hats and tails. Everyone is very excited about to-night's performance. It is the most anticipated event of the season.

In the orchestra pit, the musicians are tuning up. In the dressing rooms, the performers are being wedged

into their costumes. In the wings, the choral singers are practicing their scales. And they are all wondering the same thing: "Where is the Great Poochini?"

As the theater begins to fill, Maestro Pawvarotti, the distinguished conductor, is starting to feel very nervous.

"Where is our star?" he demands as he waves his baton wildly about.

Alas, poor Signor Poochini is still trapped, a prisoner in his own home.

"Dog-gone-it!" he howls. "I may as well be in the pound."

Deep in despair, Signor Poochini stops pacing. He cannot think anymore.

"I give up," he sighs as he sprawls across the Persian rug. "It is hopeless."

And so it seems.

There are less than thirty minutes to showtime when Signor Poochini is startled by a series of inexplicable noises in Hersh's bedroom. A light tapping followed by a loud crack; a shattering smash followed by a long, slow creak.

Signor Poochini dashes into the bedroom. When he gets there, he finds a tall figure dressed in black from head to toe, holding a flashlight. The window at his back has been smashed.

"Double horrors!" exclaims Signor Poochini. "A cat burglar!"

The intruder rudely shines his flashlight directly into Signor Poochini's eyes.

"Beat it, mutt," he snarls.

Signor Poochini stands his ground. He is wary, but unafraid.

"If you're not out of this house in three seconds, I'll snap your ears off!" he bravely barks.

The thief is infuriated. He brandishes his flashlight high above his head and approaches menacingly.

"This is your final warning, dog!" he threatens.

Signor Poochini, sensing danger, realizes that he needs to act quickly. He utters a single ferocious bark and then disappears through the bedroom door, leaving the villain alone and somewhat bewildered.

"That dog's all bark and no bite," sniggers the nasty cat burglar.

A brief moment later, the nefarious prowler is startled by a deafening blast of blaring music. He turns abruptly on his heels to locate the source of the frightening noise and is startled by a dark figure, draped in a voluminous cloak, brandishing a long sword and wearing a fancy hat.

"Battiti!"* announces the mysterious swordsman.

It is the cat burglar who now senses danger. He drops his flashlight in a flash and in a panic leaps through the window, never to return.

The gallant swordsman returns to the living-room and turns off the record player. Signor Poochini chuckles softly as he drops his French stick bread sword, doffs Hersh's old summer straw hat and removes his picnic blanket cloak.

*Fight!

Thanks to the cat burglar, the bedroom window is now open.

"The show must go on!" cries the Great Poochini as he charges through the open window.

He slips through throngs of sidewalk pedestrians and dodges speeding cars and trucks on busy flashing streets. He winds his way through dark, narrow alleyways, hurdles over high brick walls and scrambles under treacherous fences of wood and wire.

The Great Poochini finally arrives at the opera house with only seconds to spare.

"No time for grooming!" he barks as he tornadoes into his costume.

He straps on his sword to the opening strains of the overture and marches triumphantly onto the stage only to be greeted by the wild cheers of an ecstatic packed house.

Tonight, the Great Poochini is in fine fettle. His stage presence is commanding, his swordplay thrilling. And his voice . . . ah, his voice, his incomparable voice. It can move even the most cold-hearted listener to tears. When he reaches his high C, it is said that only dogs can hear him.

The audience becomes a sea of clapping paws and wagging tails as he sings the famous duet with the beautiful and enchanting diva, Madama Barkoli:

"Là ci darem la zampa
la mi dirai di sì.
Vedi, non è lontano;
partiam, ben mio, da qui."*

*There you will give me your paw, / there you will tell me "yes." / You see, it is not far; / Let us leave, my beloved.

The audience is all ears throughout the performance, and when it is over all agree that the Great Poochini's singing was nothing short of miraculous.

His loyal and devoted fans will remember tonight's performance for a very long time indeed.

And so will the Great Poochini.